Bright and Early Thursday Evening

a tangled tale

Dreamed by

Audrey Wood

Imagined by

Don Wood

HARCOURT BRACE & COMPANY

San Diego   New York   London

Requests for permission to make copies of any part of
the work should be mailed to: Permissions Department, Harcourt Brace & Company,
6277 Sea Harbor Drive, Orlando, Florida 32887-6777.

Library of Congress Cataloging-in-Publication Data
Wood, Audrey.
Bright and early Thursday evening: a tangled tale/by Audrey Wood;
illustrated by Don Wood.—1st ed.
p.   cm.
Summary: A rhyming nonsense tale featuring a series
of impossible occurrences, such as a bald-headed baby with
hair hanging over his eyes and an egg-laying rooster.
ISBN 0-15-200363-0
[1. Humorous stories. 2. Stories in rhyme.] I. Wood, Don, 1945-ill.   II. Title.
PZ8.3.W848Br   1996
[Fic]—dc20   95-37921

First edition
A   C   E   F   D   B
Printed in Singapore

The illustrations in this book were
rendered in Fractal Painter and Adobe Photoshop on a
Macintosh Power PC computer equipped with a Wacom digital art pad.
Source photographs by Don Wood, Lew Robertson, and Bruce Wood
Modeling by Angela Newman
The display type was hand-lettered by Georgia Deaver.
The text was set in Colwell.
Color separations by Bright Arts, Ltd., Singapore
Printed and bound by Tien Wah Press, Singapore
This book was printed with soya-based inks
on Nymolla Matte Art paper.
Production supervision by
Warren Wallerstein and Ginger Boyer
Designed by Lisa Peters

Dedicated to the inventors of digital art,

and to Bruce Wood, our pixel mentor

Bright and early Thursday evening,

I woke up and dreamed I was dead.

My noble red rooster laid an egg,

Then crowed till I fell out of bed.

I dressed to go to my funeral—

'Twas a simple, gala affair.

The joyful guests were weeping,

Even the poor billionaire.

When the band played "Gelatin Skeleton,"

We all sat down to dance.

Then a naked potato from Idaho

Dropped in wearing gabardine pants.

"How nice to see you again," I said

As we fell in love at first sight.

"Let's eat," said he, "I'm thirsty."

So I gobbled him down in one bite.

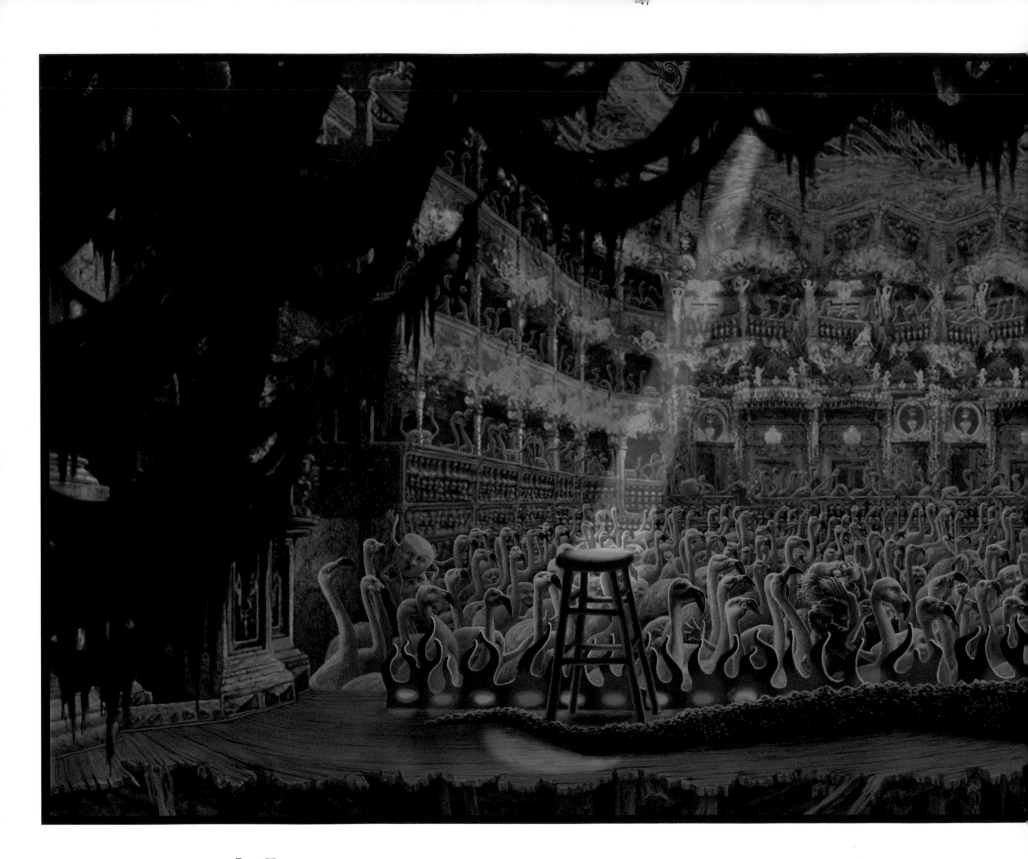

"Now you've done it!" the crocodile cried.
"That stranger was my best friend."

"I didn't do it!" I laughed in remorse.
"And I'll never do it again."

o expand my tale I'll summarize—

The potato was rescued by force.

Then the crocodile read our wedding vows,

And pronounced us single, of course.

I knew it was going to happen,
So I shouted out in surprise,

"Here comes the bald-headed baby,
With hair hanging over his eyes!"

lthough I'm a liar my story is true—

There's an end in every beginning.

So if you believe a word that I've said,

Begin again, please, at the ending.